MYSTERY SHORT STORY COLLECTION VOLUME 3

CONNOR WHITELEY

No part of this book may be reproduced in any form or by any electronic or mechanical means. Including information storage, and retrieval systems, without written permission from the author except for the use of brief quotations in a book review.

This book is NOT legal, professional, medical, financial or any type of official advice.

Any questions about the book, rights licensing, or to contact the author, please email connorwhiteley@connorwhiteley.net

Copyright © 2024 CONNOR WHITELEY

All rights reserved.

DEDICATION
Thank you to all my readers without you I couldn't do what I love.

INVITATIONS TO SECRETS, LIES AND DECEIT

2nd December 2022

Canterbury, England

No one thinks about the walls.

Before Private Eye Bettie English had fallen in love, before she had become President of The British Private Eye Federation and before she had given birth to two amazing kids, Bettie actually got a lot of cases through strange invitations. Hell, she loved it and she had gotten some of her best and most exciting cases from invitations from mystery senders.

But as she sat at a massive oak round table with only four other people she was really starting to regret her joy of receiving weird invitations.

The dining room she sat in was rather nice and almost magical in a way with beautiful red, green and bright pink tinsel hanging all over the walls and ceiling and the tinsel shined like stars off the crystal chandelier (that was probably real), Bettie had seen some impressive families do great on their Christmas decorations but this family might have topped it.

There of course wasn't one or two or even three massive pine trees in the dining room, there was one in each corner. And Bettie was amazed that each Christmas tree was decorated in an identical way with rainbow coloured LED lights gently pulsing Christmas magic, golden tinsel hugging the tree loosely and little naked candles burning on the trees filling the air with the sweet scents of frankincense and myrrh.

Bettie wasn't exactly sure why the hell these four people wanted to burn naked candles on their trees (surely they knew that was a fiery death sentence) but Bettie didn't really want to argue.

Not when she had received a very panicked letter two hours ago wanting her to attend because someone was going to die tonight.

Bettie had originally planned to spend the night with her amazing, sexy boyfriend Graham as they went through all the great (and utterly rubbish) Christmas decorations that her 70-year-old mum had given her and then Bettie was going to read her two little angels a Christmas bedtime story before she put them to bed (but them sleeping when she wanted them to was a joke at this moment. Four-month-old babies didn't like sleeping).

But the invitation had changed those plans in a flash.

"Welcome everyone," the very tall woman,

probably 32, at the head of the table said with a massive smile.

Bettie rather liked the woman's blue jeans, white shirt and shoeless feet, because it made her look normal and calm and like she was there to make sure everyone had a good time. It was just a shame that the other people at the table didn't look like that.

The other three people at the table were tall middle-aged men and wow did they look the part, and not the good or normal part, the three men were dressed in what Bettie could only describe as "grandad clothes" with their tan slacks, monocle and knitted red jumpers that looked so old they were about to fall apart.

Bettie was looking forward to seeing what these people were meeting about, and most importantly who was going to die. Something Bettie was hoping beyond hope that she could stop.

"We all know why we are here tonight," the tall woman said. "Three years ago, my father Lord Admiral Collins of the British Royal navy disappeared,"

"Happy Collins Day," the three men returned.

Bettie was shocked that she was actually attending Collins Day. She had read about it in the paper recently because his daughter, Beatrice and presumably the tall woman was her, had been launching new campaigns in search of information about her father's disappearance.

Bettie had even had a crack at the case whilst she

was on maternity leave during those extremely precious moments when her beautiful angels were finally sleeping.

The case was as strange as it got. Mr Collins had been on leave from the Navy for a month because Beatrice was getting married to the love of her life and Collins wanted to be there for the wedding and Christmas and New Year.

So he left the Naval Base at Portsmouth, England and drove to Canterbury two hours away, he kissed his wife hello and quickly popped to the shops to get some wine to celebrate his return (that was his wife's idea) and then he was never seen again.

There were no witnesses, no security footage that saw him on the second of December 2019 and his wife never heard from him again.

"Beatrice," Bettie said leaning forward, "why did your mother not get the wine?"

Everyone just looked at Bettie like she was a crazy woman.

"Who are you?" the oldest of the three men asked and Bettie noticed a minor scar under his chin like he had been punched there.

"This is Bettie English, the best private eye in the UK and somehow *she* received an invitation tonight," Beatrice said.

Bettie forced herself not to seem surprised at that comment. She was sure that if anyone had requested her presence tonight it would be Beatrice, but she certainly didn't invite Bettie with *that* tone.

"My question," Bettie said again, not really caring for the group's concern towards her.

"My mother was a woman in her late fifties who had just broken her leg after she fell down the stairs. She could barely let my father into the house let alone getting some wine," Beatrice said.

Bettie slowly nodded. That made sense.

"Nibbles Mrs Collins," a man said behind Bettie.

Bettie turned around and smiled when a very young man, maybe 19, walked in wearing a black waiter's uniform carrying a large silver tray of wine, freshly roasted nuts and smoked salmon.

Bettie loved all of those things but one part of herself she had never gotten back after her pregnancy was the ability to eat animal products. Bettie forced herself not to react to the amazing smell of the salmon despite her stomach churning.

Clearly these people didn't know about the possible death threat as the waiter placed the wine and nuts and salmon on the table and then bought out five silver plates and cutlery for them to enjoy the salmon on.

Bettie was starting to wonder if the person who actually invited her was really at the table.

"Are you not drinking Miss English?" the waiter said with concern edging his voice.

"No thank you," Bettie said. "I'm driving and I have two kids at home so I don't anymore,"

"Oh please Bettie," Beatrice said. "This wine is from the hills of Southern France, an area that my father loved. This is how we honour him on Collins Day,"

Bettie politely nodded and pretended to take a sip or two but she did not. The waiter just smiled at her and Bettie was almost a little concerned that everyone wanted her to drink. What if there was poison or something in the wine?

"What have you discovered about my father?" Beatrice asked the three men.

The youngest of the middle-aged man who Bettie was only realising now had a black eye smiled at Beatrice.

"We found one person who remembers selling your father a bottle of wine on the night in question," he said.

Bettie leant forward. "How? I didn't think the Police or Military police found anyone,"

The man with the scar under his chin sighed. "It's a great shame of our society that time loosen up tongues a lot better than a murder,"

Don't say that," Beatrice said. "My father is not dead,"

"My apologies Mrs Collins,"

That was a strange comment and now Bettie was seriously starting to wonder how the hell these people all knew each other. Bettie had believed they were friends or something but surely friends use first names and not formal surnames?

Beatrice started coughing a little and holding her stomach.

"Are you okay?" Bettie asked standing up.

Beatrice took a sip of the wine and smiled as she started picking at her salmon a little.

Bettie really wasn't liking this situation at all. She felt like a fish out of water but the mother angle was still annoying Bettie.

"Beatrice," Bettie said, "is this the same house that your mother lived in all those years ago?"

Beatrice coughed a little more and nodded before picking up a massive chunk of flaky salmon and eating it.

Bettie paced around the wooden table a little. "I assume your mother would have been in here with similar decorations when your father rang the doorbell,"

"Of course," Beatrice said grinning. "These are even the exact same decorations that were up on the night of the disappearance,"

Bettie almost felt sorry for Beatrice because she was clearly so obsessed with finding what happened to her father that Bettie was concerned she didn't have much of a life outside this hunt for the truth.

If Beatrice's mother had told the truth to the police then there was another problem, if she really had broken her leg and was on crutches then Bettie had to admit the mother was strong to walk herself all the way to the front door.

"I hadn't focused on it before," Bettie said, "but your dining room is at the back of the house and you cannot walk straight through the hallway to get from the front door to the dining room,"

Beatrice slammed her fork down on the table.

"You have to go through a number of other rooms with lots of twists and turns and this house probably has tons of hollow walls. If your mother really did that then why wasn't she more tired? And where was the waiter?"

The three men looked at Beatrice and nodded.

"You seem to be obsessed with keeping everything the same so there had to be a waiter, probably the same waiter, three years ago. Why didn't he answer the door? Or better yet, why didn't your father open the door with his front door keys?"

Beatrice downed her wine in a single gulp. "I don't know damn you. I don't know what happened to my father. I don't know what happened to my mother that night. I don't know anything,"

Bettie went over to her and folded her arms. "What do you mean you don't know what happened to your mother that night? Did she lie to the police?"

All three men stood up and went over to Beatrice. Their arms folded.

Beatrice held her stomach a little tighter. "My mother was out that night. She texted my father saying she would be home soon so he went to get the wine as a surprise,"

Bettie looked at the men. "She was having an affair, wasn't she?"

"No. No. No," Beatrice said. "That ain't true. My mummy was not having an affair,"

The last of the men that Bettie hadn't focused at all on yet just looked to the ground. And Bettie noticed his massive balding patch.

"How long did you sleep with her mother?" Bettie asked calmly.

Beatrice folded her arms and looked like she was about to cry.

"I didn't mean to sleep with her," he said not daring to look up. "I didn't mean to have sex with her. I didn't mean, well, any of it,"

Beatrice hissed a little.

"It was just my wife left me years ago, your mother was so nice and she was annoyed at the Navy for always taking her husband away from her. We were both lonely," he said.

"Damn you Jasper," Beatrice said.

Bettie went over to Jasper and gently raised his head with a single finger. "Did you kill Mr Collins?"

Jasper didn't even smile like that was a stupid thing to say, instead he simply shook his head as his eyes turned wet and Bettie knew, really knew that he was telling the truth.

Someone collapsed to the ground.

Bettie spun around.

The man with the black eye was gasping for air.

Bettie laid him perfectly straight, tried for a pulse and she didn't find one.

"Call an ambulance!" Bettie shouted.

Bettie immediately started CPR as hard and fast as she could.

Moments later the man gasped as air rushed into his lungs but he didn't open his eyes or move. But he was breathing and for now that would have to do.

Bettie picked him up and placed him gently back into his chair allowing him to lay unconscious, with his head tilted to one side so in case he vomited he wouldn't choke on it.

"I called an ambulance. They'll be here in the next hour," Beatrice said.

Bettie laughed because that really was a testament to how bad the ambulance service was getting in the UK.

"What's going on?" Jasper asked.

Bettie looked at the half-eaten plates of salmon plus her own intact plate and Bettie shook her head.

The food had to be poisoned but it also made no sense. Why poison that particular man? Why not poison Jasper or Beatrice or even herself?

Hell maybe they had poisoned Bettie.

"The waiter," Bettie said. "He smiled at me before he left and at the time I thought he was smiling at me because he knew I wasn't drinking. What if he was smiling because I was about to die?"

Beatrice shrugged. "Look at Tom's wine,"

Bettie presumed Tom was the black-eye man and Beatrice was right, Tom hadn't touched his wine so the poison hadn't come from there.

Bettie waved her hands in the air. "So I received an invitation two hours ago saying someone was going to die and they needed my help to stop it,"

"Great job you did," Beatrice said.

"Did any of you send the invitation?" Bettie asked.

The three people just looked at each other like none of them would dare do such a thing.

Bettie had to agree with them. If any of them had sent the invitation they would have known not to drink or eat or touch anything just in case poison was being used.

"So we have three problems to solve," Bettie said. "I need to know who sent me the invitation, what happened to your father and who tried to kill Tom here,"

Both Jasper, the man with the scar under the chin and Beatrice laughed.

"I'm sorry," Bettie said to the man with the scar. "What's your name?"

The man laughed. "Believe it or not, I'm the uncle of the family. Jeremiah Collins, the bum of the family who has apparently never accomplished anything in my life,"

Beatrice hissed and Bettie thought she was actually going to spit at him, there was definitely no love lost between them.

"How did you get your scar?" Bettie asked.

Bettie loved watching all the colour drain from Jeremiah's face.

"Um," he said. "I was cleaning snow off my drive two years ago and the shovel hit me,"

"We didn't have snow two years ago," Bettie

said.

"And you had that scar… three years ago but not before," Beatrice said.

"Fine," Jeremiah said trying to go for the hallway but the waiter appeared and blocked him. "I saw my brother that night he disappeared,"

"And you never said anything," Beatrice said trying to control her rage. Bettie took a few steps back just in case she lashed out.

"I was scared. I met my brother at the house that night and paid the waiter a thousand pounds the next day to say I wasn't,"

"And you still work here?" Bettie asked to the waiter.

The waiter smiled. "I love the family and I actually love the work,"

Bettie was surprised but the waiter seemed nice enough.

"I met my brother here after he found out about the affair because his wife had sent nudes to him instead of Jasper,"

Jasper looked as if he was about to die and really wanted the ground to swallow him up. Bettie loved hearing about people's secrets.

"I never wanted anything to happen but it simply turned into a massive argument. I said just divorce the woman but he didn't believe in divorce,"

"So you kept pressing daddy and he swung at you," Beatrice said as she rubbed her left arm.

"When did the argument happen? Before or after

he went out to get the wine?" Bettie asked.

"After and we never drunk the wine. He was saving it for the wife,"

Bettie was glad these people were revealing their secrets to her because at least the night of the 2nd December 2019 was starting to make sense.

Mr Collins travelled home after deployment to find his home empty and his wife said she was on her way back so he goes out to get a bottle of wine, then Collins received a series of nude photos of his wife that wasn't meant for him and he suddenly realises she was having an affair.

Yet Bettie couldn't understand another question now, what had happened to the wine?

"I need to speak to your mother," Bettie said to Beatrice with a lot more force than she intended to.

Beatrice looked at the ground. "You can't. She's… fragile. She isn't right in the head. And she… isn't a fan of Collins Day,"

"My boyfriend is a cop. One call from me and he will come running and he will investigate all of this including the assault from Jeremiah, the affair and everything else," Bettie said.

Beatrice stood up perfectly straight so Bettie knew there was more secrets to uncover but she believed that everyone was allowed to have at least secrets to themselves. Hell she certainly did.

"I took her to a home yesterday," Beatrice said. "She has advanced dementia for the past year and a half. She kept thinking that the waiter was my father and, nothing has been going well for her,"

Well that was another dead end for the case.

Bettie just looked at poor unconscious Tom and really hoped that when the ambulance and paramedics got here she could have them run a little test for her.

She needed to know exactly what poison had tried to kill Tom.

Yet Bettie was still no closer to knowing who had wanted her here tonight, who had tried to kill Tom and most importantly what had happened to Mr Collins.

***

Bettie's boyfriend Graham had to be the sexiest man alive and she seriously loved Senior Scientist Zoey Quill because she had agreed to go late into the lab tonight to run a few tests for Bettie, Bettie was definitely going to have to buy Zoey and her husband and her children a very special present for Christmas.

A few hours later, Bettie was sitting at the wooden table again with Beatrice, Jasper and Jeremiah with the air still smelling of fresh salmon, freshly roasted pecans and strong bitter coffee that the waiter had just bought out when her phone buzzed with the test results.

There was no way in hell that Bettie could even pronounce or read the name of the toxin used against Tom but thankfully (and because Zoey was so amazing) she had included a layman's version of the toxin.

"A very rare nerve agent was placed into the

salmon tonight," Bettie said. "And this particular nerve agent has to be programmed with the DNA of the victim before it activates,"

"So we're safe?" Jasper and Jeremiah asked at the same time.

Bettie nodded but was still a little surprised that Jeremiah was Beatrice's uncle yet she had been hissing, coughing and holding her stomach all night like she had been poisoned.

"What's wrong with your stomach?" Bettie asked knowing that she really needed to get answers now.

Beatrice looked past Bettie and weakly at the young waiter. Bettie didn't know whether to be concerned or not that it was fair to say the waiter had gotten Beatrice pregnant.

"That's why you stay as the waiter," Bettie said. That made a lot of sense but the nerve agent could only have come from one source that was possible for Bettie to understand.

The waiter went over, stood next to Beatrice and kissed her. And it was nice to see that they were in true love and not some fling that had ended in a pregnancy.

"Did your father ever bring back things from the Navy?" Bettie asked.

Beatrice held the waiter's hand so tight that her knuckles had turned white. "Yes, he bought back little things but he always kept them locked in a safe,"

Bettie just laughed because she finally realised what was going on, how someone had tried to kill

Tom and what had happened to Mr Collins three years ago.

Someone, not Mr Collins, was living in the walls.

"Have you ever heard sounds in the walls?" Bettie asked. "Have you ever heard sounds like someone was walking about at night?"

Beatrice's eyes widened. "My mother... she said someone pushed her down the stairs when she broke her leg I never believed her. I lied about when she broke her leg but she did break it four months before my father disappeared,"

"And my brother constantly moaned about food going missing," Jeremiah said. "Nothing weird has happened for years though. No food or anything,"

Bettie just nodded. "This old house has a lot of hollow spaces in-between the walls and I think if we open up some of these walls then we'll find something very disturbing,"

"You think... my daddy's inside?" Beatrice said.

Bettie took out her phone and called Graham. She didn't have the heart to agree with Beatrice but they did need a team of crime scene techs here immediately.

There was a lot of answers to find. No matter how disturbing they might be.

***

The constant low sounds of crime scene techs in their white uniforms, police sirens and Beatrice and the two remaining men giving statements filled the air as Bettie stood there outside in the icy cold winter night with her beautiful sexy Graham standing next to her.

Thankfully he was wearing a massive thick coat that Bettie clung to in case it would warm her up, Bettie was just glad that their little angels were asleep with Bettie's nephew Sean and his boyfriend harry watching over them. At least they were warm and toasty tonight.

Despite all the police cars and white crime scene vans outside, Bettie was still pleased that Beatrice's house looked beautiful and Christmassy outside as it had earlier with plenty of gravity-defying light displays in the shapes of angels, reindeer and snowmen. It was like you were about to walk into a winter wonderland.

And not a house filled with lies, deceit and secrets.

Graham's phone buzzed, took it out and gasped before showing the photo to Bettie. Bettie was amazed that the crime scene techs had found an entire network of narrow spaces in-between the old walls with remains of food wrappings, matches and water bottles littered throughout.

Yet the photo was of the perfectly mummified body of Mr Collins who was wrapped up tightly in a tarp and stuffed at the end of one of the passages that the person living inside the walls had made for themselves.

Bettie felt so disgusted because it was flat out wrong for someone to live inside the walls instead of living in their own house. The things this person could have seen was a horrific invasion of privacy but at least it explained a lot.

It explained why Beatrice's mother had said a man pushed her down the stairs, it explained why Mr Collins' brother didn't know what had happened to his brother after he left and what had happened to the wine, and it finally explained what happened to Mr Collins the night of the 2nd December 2019.

"What do you think happened that night?" Graham asked as he finished texting the crime scene techs because apparently the scene was far too busy, fragile and chaotic to risk Graham contaminating it.

"I think the man or woman came out the walls looking for food that night. He found Mr Collins angry and frustrated about his wife's affair and Mr Collins caught him or her. There was a fight and Mr Collins died," Bettie said.

"Then the killer took him into the walls to avoid anyone finding the body. But just imagine living with your own murder victim for so long?" Graham asked.

Bettie just laughed. "Babe, you realise what we do for a living. And you think a man living in the walls is the weirdest?"

"Fair point," Graham said, kissing her on the head.

"But where is the man or woman now?" Bettie asked. "And we know what happened to Mr Collins but what happened to Tom and who invited me?"

"Detective!" a uniformed officer standing by the

police tape shouted to Graham and then the officer gestured to a man engulfed in the shadow of the bright streetlamps.

Graham waved him through and Bettie instantly knew who this man was. He was the man living in the walls.

Bettie just stared at the very, almost dangerously thin man walk towards them, he was clean-shaved, in good health and looked rather handsome for a man in his late fifties.

The man was wearing black jogging bottoms, a very nice red t-shirt and a thick puffer jacket that suited him perfectly.

"Why kill him?" Bettie asked. Graham didn't seem to be following.

"I never meant to do that Miss English," the man said. "I was made homeless after my divorce and I had nothing but I was once a bricklayer and my father worked on this house,"

"So you knew about the gaps in the wall," Bettie said.

"Of course and my father was a cowboy builder. He didn't put in any insulation or anything so it was hardly a health hazard,"

"It's still illegal," Graham said.

Bettie waved him silent and gestured the man to continue.

"I knew the family always celebrated their silly little Collins Day tonight so I wanted... I wanted someone to finally discover the truth, because, he keeps talking to me,"

Bettie hugged the man for some reason she didn't understand but she could tell that he wasn't a bad person, he was just a man that had been forced by a situation to react.

Granted Bettie never would have decided to live in the walls of a house if she was homeless, but she could understand if someone was desperate enough.

"I never meant to kill Mr Collins but he caught me and I hate living with that corpse anyway. Please arrest me. At least you guys have heating, meals and free water. You have any idea how annoying it is having to wake up in the middle of the night just to get a day's supply of water,"

Bettie smiled and shook her head as Graham cuffed the man and arrested him for murder.

"Why did you try to kill Tom? You must have seen where Mr Collins kept the illegal things we bought back from the Navy and programmed the nerve agent," Bettie said.

The man's smile deepened. "I never wanted to kill Tom. I was aiming for Beatrice. I didn't know you needed to programme the nerve agent so that only means one thing, doesn't it Miss English?"

Bettie waved Graham so he took the man over to the nearest police car and Bettie was just shocked at yet another secret this family held. Mr Collins had programmed the nerve agent to kill Tom before he died, Bettie wasn't even sure she wanted to know why Mr Collins wanted to kill him (maybe he believed it was Tom who was having the affair with the wife) but Bettie knew one thing for sure.

She was really glad that the man, whoever he was, had invited her tonight so she could uncover the secrets, lies and deceptions that had been eating this family away for so long. And now, hopefully, just hopefully Beatrice could find some peace and move on from Collins Day.

And as Bettie went home to kiss her two little angels goodnight, she really hoped that was true. Because she had seen first-hand the sheer cost of people not being able to move on from the past.

It never ended well and it never led to a happy Christmas.

DEATH FOR THE WIFE
11ᵗʰ December 2022
Unknown Location, Southeast England

Assassin Eva Longleat had never ever been somewhere as cold and freezing and icy as the southeast of England today. Normally she was off killing, singing and dancing in Spain or wonderful France or even sunny Egypt, but a job was a job and she sadly had to return to her birth country to kill a new target.

Eva stood behind a thick, dense oak tree without any leaves at the very edge of the massive field sloping on a hill as she pressed herself against the tree becoming one with it in order to better avoid detection. But it was so cold that her breath was forming thick columns of vapour like a dragon in front of her, and it was so cold that Eva actually felt the icy cold air coat her lungs along with the sweet amazing aromas of wild garlic, rosemary and thyme.

Maybe at the end of the job Eva would pick some for herself as a little treat.

That was just such an uncomfortable feeling and clearly Eva needed to get a damn slight better at reading weather reports, the weather stations had it was going to be freezing but she hadn't listened. English weather stations weren't exactly renowned for their accuracy after all.

Eva loved how the little frost-covered blades of grass sparkled like diamonds against the rising early morning sun that looked like a weak little beacon of hope through the dense, ugly fog and mist that veiled the field.

Eva shivered a little more as she struggled to remain warm, and wished she was wearing another thick arctic coat on top of the white one she was already wearing, and she could barely feel her toes through her army issue boots, thermal trousers and other military-grade pieces of kit she always carried on jobs.

This job should have been easier because the husband who was an English Lord had hired Eva to kill his wife because she had been giving his money to terrorists, drug dealers and communists so he had wanted his wife stopped. Normally that wouldn't be enough for someone to dare call Eva but she was very interested in when the husband mentioned his wife was meeting a group today.

A group of women dedicated to the burning down of the police, abortion centres and any charities dedicated to helping the unholy gay abominations.

It was a flat out weird ideology but Eva had secretly scanned the husband's and wife's electronics, stalked them during the night and day and amazingly enough the husband was clean and the wife was extremely guilty.

If anyone had actually had the balls to ask Eva, she almost wanted not to kill these women because surely they were only a little misguided? Surely they couldn't be all bad and corrupted and wanted other women to suffer?

But Eva knew that was a lie and these women were most certainly beyond help.

Eva had already watched the wife brutally attack a doctor that gave women perfectly safe abortions, and when Eva had tried to save the woman after the wife had left, Eva had sadly found the woman was already dead.

So as far as Eva was concerned the wife just had to die, but of course she still accepted the two million pound "donation" for her time. She was always happy that HMRC taxed her as an escort rather than the more illegal hitwoman.

"Today sisters we are here,"

The voice carried through the dense fog very well and Eva just focused on the field ahead of her and frowned at what she saw.

There had to be at least ten women dressed in very thin white sheets, probably meant to show their virginity, gathered in a wide circle centred about one single woman that really had to die.

The wife's name was Paisley Oasson, she was probably about five-five, very slim and had no very special abilities about herself that would make her dangerous. She didn't go to the gym, she wasn't a fighter but she did have a very commanding voice.

Eva focused on Paisley's long artic white hair that was blowing gently in the freezing air that was coming from the River Medway a few hundred metres away.

"Today is the day all of you take the vow to me of service, loyalty and hope for a more equal future,"

Paisley said.

Eva just laughed. The wife was even more stupid than she ever thought possible, Eva had no idea how burning down police stations, charities and abortion centres would help make the world more equal for women but clearly this Paisley nob thought it would.

Eva knelt down on the frost-covered ground and started setting up her sniper rifle.

She had considered using her great throwing knives, her wonderful pistol or her massive axe, but she didn't want to give Paisley a chance to escape her.

Eva needed to kill everyone around her too, so maybe she should have used her machine gun actually but it was too late for that now.

"And now we sacrifice the interloper to myself," Paisley said.

Eva instantly froze and heard three sets of footprints coming through the forest behind her.

There was Paisley, the ten women with her and the three walking through the forest. That was a lot of people to kill and Eva was going to have to act fast.

Eva quickly finished setting up her sniper rifle and decided she just had to climb up the massive pine next to her.

It wasn't ideal with the trees having no leaves but it would have to work for now at least.

Eva went up the tree, preached herself on a massive branch and took out her sniper rifle, aiming it in the direction of Paisley.

The problem was the fog and mist were far too thick for Eva to see clearly. She would be shooting blind.

Eva reached towards her back for her sniper rifle casing so she could get out her heat-vision scope but she couldn't. She had left the casing on the ground.

Eva leant over the edge of the branch and frowned when she saw three women shivering in white robes kicking her casing.

It was so tempting just to shoot all the women where they stood but Eva couldn't risk the noise at the moment. She had also sadly forgotten to add her silencer in all the chaos of climbing the tree.

But thankfully sniper rifles also made very good clubs to smash skulls in.

Eva carefully stood up on the branch and leapt down to the ground.

She landed on one of the women. Snapping her neck.

Eva whipped out her sniper rifle.

Swinging it. Whacking one woman with it. Teeth flew out. Blood melted frost.

Eva rushed over to her.

Jumping on her head.

Her skull shattered.

The last woman tackled Eva to the ground.

She slammed her fists into Eva.

Eva blocked her other punches.

The woman punched Eva in the boob.

Eva hissed. She tried to slash the woman with her nails.

The woman blocked it.

The woman shouted for help.

Eva headbutted the woman.

The woman fell to the ground.

Eva snapped her neck.

Eva jumped up and was about to run back up the tree when she saw the ten women in white robes were walking towards her holding little black pistols all aimed at her.

Normally Eva would have set off a smoke grenade, told some silly story about her childhood to buy her some time or just do something to help herself, but she couldn't or didn't.

Eva only stood there and focused on her target as she came over to her like Paisley didn't have a care in the world.

Eva just needed to wait for the perfect moment to strike because she had dealt with cults before and the key was always killing the leader.

The cultists or whatever these women were too dedicated to Paisley not to try to kill Eva given the chance but Eva knew, just knew there would be a few seconds after Paisley died to attack the followers.

The advantages of them grieving too much for their awful leader.

"I was like you once," Paisley said. "I was a woman who believed in equality, murderer abortionists and that I was as good as any man,"

Eva just laughed because this really was the biggest amount of bullshit she had ever heard. She would like to see a man kill Paisley like she was hopefully going to and climb trees as easily as she did.

"But the world is changing," Paisley said as she stood within touching distance of Eva. "Men are strong, powerful and divine beings that need the support of women behind them,"

Eva noticed that a lot of the ten women were focusing completely on Paisley's so-called divine words and they were mostly forgetting about Eva so she only needed to wait a little longer so the followers were completely disarmed.

Eva just hoped that would be sooner rather than

later as she really couldn't feel her toes anymore and even her fingers were starting to become less flexible.

Eva wasn't even sure if she could form a fist anymore. That was how freezing she was.

"It is not the job of women to outdo men. Men are the divine beings and the fated rulers of women so we must help them. Long Live Mankind, death to womankind," Paisley said.

"Love live mankind, death to womankind," everyone returned.

Eva shot forward. She had had enough of this bullshit.

She grabbed Paisley. Throwing her against a tree.

A small branch shot through Paisley's eyes. Blood poured all over the snow.

She was still alive.

Eva kicked Paisley's head. Forcing the small branch through her eye and into her brain.

Eva ripped the body off the branch and her eyeball was still attached to the branch.

Paisley was dead.

The followers screamed.

Eva grabbed her sniper rifle.

She smashed one of them round the head.

Blood splashed against snow.

Eva rushed over to her corpse. Grabbing her pistol.

Eva shot the other followers.

They were all screaming. Dying. Suffering.

Eva shot them all in the head as she finished making sure every single one of these foul women were dead and could never ever spread their hateful ideology to anyone else.

When all fourteen corpses of the women were

lying on the ground, some without any teeth, all of them with bullet holes in their heads and all of their hearts had stopped beating, Eva just frowned at all of them.

Eva never wanted to kill these people but they had made her. Eva had actually wanted these people to live and maybe they could see the errors of their ways but they were never going to do that.

And Eva had always known that, she had been an assassin for too long not to know that the people she was hired to kill were always far too gone to be helped. But it was still a great shame because Paisley could have done so much good with her husband's money, she could have built schools in Africa, helped the homeless and helped women flee domestic violence.

But she hadn't chosen that path and as Eva pressed her army boots down on Paisley's skull listening to it crack under her weight, Eva just knew exactly what she had to do now. The husband had paid Eva two million pounds to kill his wife and now Eva just had to use that money for good.

Just like the wife should have done.

So Eva picked up all her shell casings despite picking up the metal casings being extremely painful in the arctic conditions, and she simply disappeared from the crime scene.

And she went off to get warm, toasty and to donate a damn lot of money to a lot of great charities and Eva was really looking forward to that. She was actually looking forward to doing some good a lot more than she ever wanted to admit to anyone, let alone herself.

NEVER GETTING BACK TOGETHER

Detective Jason Jenkins absolutely loved walking up the narrow little road of his ex-boyfriend's. It was always the same and it was great to see that nothing had changed since they had broken up. All the semi-detached houses with their bright orange bricks were still the same, the windows were always clean and all the little front gardens were perfectly done.

Jason was hardly impressed that the damn pavement was still as lumpy, chipped and filled with little holes as it always had. He wanted to focus on the houses and the neighbourhood but he couldn't because a rogue chip in the pavement might take him out.

When it was really cold his silly left knee still got sore because of a fall he had had when him and his ex had been carrying too many bags of shopping and had fallen off the pavement. Those damn chips and holes in the pavement were just lethal as far as Jason was concerned.

Jason shook the stupid memory away and he smiled at the sweet aromas of cherry, apple and blueberry pies that filled the air as he went past one house. It looked exactly like all the others but he had always liked the woman who lived there.

Ms Oliver was a wonderful lady and Jason had loved talking to her when in the evening and even baking with her when his ex had working late. She was a great woman and Jason was definitely going to catch up with her later on.

He was impressed to see some of the homeowners had decided to plant some roses and lavender, but they were the minority. Everyone else seemed just to be the exact same, but then again Jason really understood that people didn't have the time to focus on their gardens these days.

He would have loved to spend more time in his own garden, attending to his flowers, vegetables and some exotic plants that his current boyfriend Felix had brought him on his travels around the world as a leading banker. Jason really did love Felix, he was just perfect, wonderful and hot as hell.

It was just a shame that being a detective was such a job at times but Jason wouldn't have changed anything for the world. He loved helping people, putting criminals behind bars and just making the world a more just place.

When he got to the end of the street Jason frowned as he reached the dead end where his ex-boyfriend lived. The semi-detached house was exactly the same with its bright orange bricks as everyone else but the rusting black SUV on the drive told him his ex hadn't changed.

Jason hated that his Superintendent had "gifted" him the honour of answering the 999 call. He hadn't wanted to do it and he really wished he had passed it on to someone else but the call had been deemed serious enough to not be fake but not serious enough for a patrol officer to respond to, so Jason had sadly been given the short straw.

It was even worse that he had literally finished a robbery case about an hour ago and for once there weren't any new cases lined up for him. Now he really wished there had been.

"I didn't expect you to come," a woman said.

Jason looked to his left and saw his ex-boyfriend's sister Elena was walking towards him. She still looked as amazing as she always did with her white blouse, blue tennis shoes and black trousers that made her look a million dollars. Her husband might have been a lucky man, but Jason wasn't sure.

"I didn't expect to be given the call to respond to," Jason said. "Do you know what happened?"

Elena shrugged. "Called and told me to get over here immediately and it was important,"

Jason laughed. His ex had always liked saying those types of stupid things when they were together when all he really wanted was sex and Jason just wanted to work.

Jason went over to the brown wooden door and

knocked on it.

It was already open.

Jason rolled his eyes because this might have been serious after all so he took out his baton and got Elena to stand behind him.

Jason opened the door and was immediately overwhelmed by the smell of rich, greasy KFC. It was a sensational smell that Jason flat out loved but his ex didn't like chicken for a reason he never shared. He never would have had KFC in his house.

Jason went along the short blue hallway with a staircase, living room and bathroom all jetting out from it.

The bathroom was clean, that was surprising enough in itself, and Jason checked the small living room. He couldn't believe it was still as cosy as it always was with the massive TV on the wall, the small black sofa him and his ex used to cuddle up on in the evening and the glass cabinets along the far wall that housed all sorts of weird little items they had bought together on their trips.

Jason had loved those trips and he was surprised his ex had kept them after all this time.

His ex wasn't in the room though.

Jason went through a small archway towards the kitchen with its chrome finishings. The chrome worktops were sterile, there wasn't even a loaf of bread on the side and everything was positioned like his ex had never lived here.

Jason even checked the little chrome kettle and

just as he had guessed, it was empty of water something his ex had never done. Someone had gone through the ground floor at the very least and cleaned everything.

"Don't touch anything else," Jason said to Elena. "I think a forensic team are going to be needed,"

Elena folded her arms. "What's happening? Where's my brother?"

"I don't know," Jason said, "but I need to know what time did he call you?"

"15:00. That's one hour ago. You cannot clean any entire house forensically or whatever you said within an hour, surely?"

Jason couldn't disagree even the professional crew his friends worked for couldn't do a house that quickly. He wasn't sure what that meant except there was a chance that the call to Elena was fake or his ex was a part of this criminal plot.

"Do you ever say his name?" Elena asked.

Jason laughed. "No, I just refer to him as the *Ex*,"

"He did love you, you know, and his name is Jack,"

Jason nodded. He had loved Jack too but Jack didn't respect him, care about his career or give a damn about him being a cop and what that meant. It had been Jason finding the coke stash in Jack's garage that had broken him.

He just couldn't be dealing with that whilst being a cop.

"He's clear too, has been for about a year," Elena said.

Jason nodded and went up the little staircase towards the three bedrooms. The landing still smelt of wonderful KFC but the air was colder up here and Jason really wasn't sure why the taste of warm chicken was forming on his tongue. Jack hated chicken, he would never let it in the house.

Jason went into the two spare rooms and they were as filled with crap as they always had been. Jason had never understood how Jack could find so much crap to fill cardboard box after box and perfectly organise it in the spare rooms.

Then Jason went into the master bedroom, his old room, and he just hissed as it looked exactly the same. The massive Queen-sized bed still had the delightfully soft white sheets that Jason had really enjoyed making love to Jack in, the white chest of draws and the in-built wardrobe were both still there and they looked as French and perfect as they always did.

Even the immense floor-to-ceiling windows that went out onto a small balcony area that just wasn't practical at all were still perfectly clean.

"He couldn't bring himself to change it," Elena said. "I wanted him to but he just couldn't,"

"Where is he?" Jason asked. "We've searched the entire house and we have to make sure he's okay,"

Jason was surprised he cared that much but he just wanted his ex to be okay, safe and alive. He didn't care about the past and he didn't care what had happened between them, he just wanted, needed Jack to be okay.

There was movement out on the landing.

Jason went to turn around but Elena gasped and Jason felt the cold metal barrel of a gun press against the back of his head.

"Move over there," a woman said.

Jason went to the other side of the bedroom and frowned as he focused on the awful woman with the Glock. She wasn't that tall but in her long black trench coat, floppy hat and high heels, Jason couldn't deny she looked scary as hell.

She sort of had that professional sexy assassin vibe to her that Jason had heard a lot of straight men talk about over the years, but never really understood it until now.

"Where is Jack?" the woman asked.

"I was hoping you could tell me that," Jason said really wanting to know himself.

"I broke in earlier to find him and then I was about to drive away when I noticed you two come in. I thought you might know what was happening," the woman said.

"Who are you?" Elena asked.

"Oh of course how rude of me. My name is Sophie Cliffe, Jack's ex-girlfriend. It seems he went bisexual after you dumped him but he dumped me and I do not take no for an answer,"

"So what's your plan?" Jason asked. "Wait for

him to come home and then torture him until he loves you,"

Jason shook his head as the damn woman nodded. He didn't love Jack any more but he didn't want him to suffer, he wasn't a monster. All he wanted was for Jack to be okay but Jason knew that was impossible if Sophie got to him first.

"We don't know where he is," Jason said, "but if we go downstairs and make each other a cup of tea I am sure he will be back shortly,"

"There's no teabags sorry," Sophie said.

"Why?" Elena asked taking a step closer.

"Because I am a paid assassin by trade and I like cleaning a house. I find it relaxing to get rid of a person's identity and DNA after I kill them, but I started cleaning early and I never liked his teabags,"

"Same," Jason said hoping to build a rapport with her. "They have a weird bitter taste to them don't they?"

"Totally," Sophie said taking a few steps towards Jason.

Jason so badly wanted to jump her but he wasn't sure. He wanted to defeat her, to save Elena and Jack but he wanted a little more information first. If he could make her confess to a bunch of murders then there might even be a chance of him making homicide one day.

"Have you killed anyone famous or wouldn't I have heard of you before?" Jason asked.

Sophie laughed. "Detective Jason Jenkins I am so

good at my job that I never leave a body behind. I never get caught and all my victims are officially missing persons so I will always be okay. Unlike you,"

Jason forced himself not to take a step back as she came closer to him. Elena looked like she was going to make a move but Jason shook his head.

She didn't listen. She jumped forward.

Sophie aimed at her.

Jason leapt forward.

Tackling Sophie to the ground.

Climbing on top of her.

He punched her in the face.

Sophie swung the gun around.

She kicked him.

Jason flew off her.

Elena was whacked across the face.

Sophie leapt up.

She aimed the gun at Elena.

Jason went to charge at her.

Sophie waved the gun around.

Elena leapt forward.

Jason did the same.

The gun went off.

Everyone stopped and then Jason noticed she had fired it into the ceiling and Sophie was now heading towards the door.

"When I find Jack we will be together and then I will make him watch me kill you both so he knows never to leave me again," Sophie said.

A fist shot out from the hallway and knocked

Sophie out cold.

Jason knew it was Jack and his stomach just tightened into a painful knot as he realised he was going to have to talk to his exboyfriend. Something he seriously didn't want to do but Jason certainly deserved an explanation into what the hell just happened.

***

Thankfully, Jason was seriously pleased that it had only taken backup an hour to arrive, process the scene and take all of their witness statements. Some bigshots of MI6 had turned up to take away Sophie because she was a major international assassin that had killed in over twenty countries and that gave the UK power over its allies and enemies. Jason didn't even pretend to understand what was happening on the political front.

He was really glad that Elena and Jack were both okay and they were both sitting on the little black sofa in the living room. The entire house was silent, stunk of KFC and was nice and warm now that Jack had turned on the heating.

Jason liked how all the police presence had gone back to the station so he was alone with his ex and his ex's sister. There was nothing awkward about that at all but Jason was glad to see Jack again. His typical gym body with his broad shoulders, sexy thin waist and beautiful biceps were amazing to see again, but this was lust.

It wasn't love and Jason realised that maybe it

had never been, but that was okay.

Jack had explained how Sophie had been after him as a cover and when her missing to kill someone in the town had been complete, she had told him everything because she wanted to give it all up.

Jack had rejected her because he didn't want to be with a liar, an assassin or a fake. He just wanted to be loved and that was something Sophie could never give him because Jason was certain she had no idea how to. It was a shame but Jason doubted anything could ever be done for someone as weird as Sophie.

And the KFC smell was because Jack loved chicken now, he always ate it in different ways and he was trying to explore his horizons instead of being the single-minded man he had been when Jason had loved him.

Jason was really glad Jack was trying.

"I have to go but lovely seeing you again Jason," Elena said.

Jason hugged her. "You too, don't be a stranger,"

Elena nodded and gave him a gentle kiss on the cheek and then it was just Jason and Jack in the living room together.

"I always did love our times together," Jack said. "I might have been a dick you to you but I did love you,"

"I know but just like you and Sophie, we are never getting back together," Jason said as carefully as he could.

"I know but your boyfriend's lucky as hell. I saw

you post about him on social media a few times,"

Jason smiled. He had forgotten he still hadn't deleted Jack from his social media accounts, but maybe he wouldn't, maybe there was just no point.

"I know we can't get together," Jack said. "but I wouldn't mind being friends and getting to know you again. Would you like that?"

Jason smiled because he could see his ex had changed, he could see how much kinder, helpful and wonderful Jack was these days, and Jason had always liked being friends with his exes.

And his boyfriend was still away on business for another few days so a single night of talking, catching up and watching TV would hardly be a bad thing and everyone could always use more friends.

Jason nodded and sat on the little black sofa without cuddling up with Jack. It felt weird at first but after they started talking it soon turned into laughter and it was like they had never been a part and they had always been friends.

Exactly how he liked it and this new wonderful friendship had only been possible because a man and a psychotic assassin that were never getting back together. It was weird as hell but Jason couldn't argue how great the end result was.

ASSASSIN PROBLEMS

As far as Grace Zouch was concerned, it was simply natural, right and just for all assassins to have some kind of moral code. She had never really spoken to other assassins about it because all assassins just seemed to have one, and her one was simple.

Don't kill innocent people.

As Grace stared out of the massive, perfectly clean floor-to-ceiling windows of her modern art-of-the-state kitchen high-rise apartment in the heart of London, she found that if she simply lived by that rule then almost everything in life was perfect and things would sort themselves out.

Grace liked watching the crowds of Chinese tourists, busy London commuters and all the other young people walking up and down the snaking streets of London. It was calming to see them all in their different hats, heights and weights just walking about peacefully, being none the wiser about the dangerous games that were being played through

London.

The snaking streets below had metal and glass and even a white plastic high rise building lining the street. Grace didn't like the new modern buildings popping up everywhere but the modern buildings, unlike the old ones, weren't designed with assassins in mind.

They were always so much easier to break into and kill people in.

There was a particular group of young men and women crossing the wide black road that caught her attention. They were all holding hands, clearly in love and they were enjoying the sites. Grace really wanted that sort of love but being an assassin was a lonely job sadly. She wanted a relationship but she just had to wait a little longer.

As much as it pained her.

Grace forced herself to look away from the wonderful modern world outside because she had a problem and she couldn't solve it by looking outside.

She had always liked the kitchen. It didn't matter where she was in the world or the time period, if she had access to a good kitchen then she knew in the end everything would be alright. Grace had always loved cooking, baking and simply creating a beautiful dish out of small dull ingredients.

Even now Grace loved the great aromas of curry powder, egg and a whole range of rich, earthy spices from this morning's breakfast that made the sensational flavour of chicken curry form on her tongue. She really did love cooking.

Grace ran her hand across the perfectly smooth and slightly cold grey marble kitchen island. Her small laptop was just staring back at her and Grace really needed to solve her problem now.

She had been hired to assassinate an awful man by the name of Ellis Hull, a former religious leader who had ended up creating a cult. Grace normally didn't care too much about cults because they were just crazies that stayed put most of the time, but Ellis's cult was extreme.

They had already been connected to over a hundred murders in London over the past decade and whilst the individual cult members got charged and arrested, Ellis always walked away scot-free.

Grace had noticed that the murder victims were always white, young women who were walking home in the evening. The latest murder had been 9 pm and the earliest had been 6 pm, that wasn't a great amount of room to kill someone but Grace had managed to do it all in less time.

Ellis was clearly pulling the strings here but Grace just had no idea how to get to him. He never left his apartment that was directly below her and he had sealed the apartment up tight.

Grace would have loved to simply drill down into his apartment, kill him and then escape. Or better yet simply blow up her own apartment so Ellis would be caught in the blast.

But he had sealed and reinforced his apartment

and the dead building owner had only confirmed her suspicions about Ellis not being scared to kill people.

Sadly the police hadn't managed to connect him to that murder either.

Grace looked at her laptop and clicked on the blueprints of the building again. All the vents, air-conditioning units and the windows were reinforced and protected beyond what Grace had ever seen before. Even the really powerful corrupt businesspeople she normally killed didn't have this level of protection.

So why did Ellis?

Grace folded her arms and paced round the kitchen island for a moment. The wonderful aroma and taste of the curry made her smile and the slight chill of the floor made her shiver slightly.

Ellis couldn't have built this all for himself because he didn't have any enemies that would warrant this kind of extreme reaction. So Grace couldn't help but wonder what if all of this reinforcement was to stop Ellis from escaping?

Grace grinned because that was a hell of a realisation and that changed everything. If that was true then Ellis might have *once* been the cult leader and the murderer but not any more. What if there was a new cult leader that was hiding behind Ellis to conduct their criminal deeds?

Grace went back over to her laptop and double-checked who had hired her to kill Ellis. She deep dived into the name, the account that paid her and after spending an hour deep diving, she found that the name was fake.

Someone wanted Ellis dead but they weren't who they said they were. Grace just shook her head because that meant the real cult leader had hired her to kill him and they were wanting to come into the light after Ellis's death.

Grace wasn't sure what to do now. She knew she couldn't just let the new cult leader reveal themselves and come into the light, that would only cause even more people to die, but she couldn't allow Ellis to live because he deserved punishment for his own murders.

She was going to have to kill them both.

Grace couldn't believe she was going to have to do this but she went into her massive bedroom, put on a flowery delivery uniform and she picked up a few guns to be on the safe side.

Then she went out of her apartment.

Grace might have lived in a high-rise but she had never really understood the weird little narrow corridors. The dirty white paint was starting to flake off in places and the blue carpet tiles were just awful as was the minor urine smell that filled the air.

She hooked a right in the too-warm metal staircase with even more dirty white painted walls and she went down to Ellis's floor.

It was only now she was realising she really should have picked up some flowers given she was a flower delivery girl without any flowers. She wanted to kick herself but she couldn't change things now, she was committed for a change.

She went out into another weird little narrow corridor and went to the very end of the corridor where a heavy metal door was. It was Ellis's room and Grace doubted she could get inside without a blowtorch and at least an hour. The door looked that thick, strong and stupid in a place like this.

Grace pounded on the door and a moment later the thick door fell open and a young woman popped out.

She sort of looked beautiful with her long black hair, her white dress and the blood that covered her hand was an interesting touch that Grace wanted to appreciate later on but she couldn't right now.

Grace and the woman just looked at each other for a moment. Grace was tempted to kill or attack or punch the woman immediately but there was a gentleness and kindness in the woman's eyes that she hadn't seen for ages.

And Grace realised the woman was checking her out, and Grace couldn't deny the woman was fairly hot in return.

"Did you want to come in before someone sees the blood on my hand?" the woman asked.

"Only if you don't kill me," Grace said.

"Why would I ever do that Grace Zouch?" the woman asked.

Grace just laughed as she followed the hot woman inside, of course the damn hottie would know her name and Grace had no idea who the woman was but she was excited as hell to find out.

Ellis's apartment was hardly that bad considering he was a cult leader and a prisoner. There was only a living room, a bathroom and a bedroom in the entire place with a sort of makeshift kitchen tucked away in one corner.

Grace didn't like the living room much. She hated how strange satanic, cultic symbols lined two entire walls and with skulls, blood samples and human hair decorating it.

Even the blood red sofas were about to fall apart and Grace couldn't understand why Ellis's cold dead body was covered in shattered glass from the coffee table. It wasn't a very clean kill, it wasn't very effective and now people would be asking too many questions.

It was why Grace had always preferred poison when it actually came down to the kill, it was hard to trace and if a target had previous medical conditions then it was simple to get away with the murder.

But it was the refreshing scents of coffee, vanilla and wine that got Grace interested in the murder. The slightly bitter taste of coffee formed on her tongue and she was convinced that this woman had tried to seduce him to kill him.

That was clever and extremely cold.

"He attacked me," the woman said but Grace could tell she was lying.

"No he didn't," Grace said. "The idiot didn't even know what hit him because you somehow got in here and you kill him before he could react,"

"I didn't kill him actually, the glass shards that rammed themselves into his lungs killed him,"

Grace laughed. If that was the way this hottie wanted to play then Grace was going to enjoy this a lot.

"You tried to seduce him I take it," Grace said.

"Of course he's a middle-aged man that someone kept locked up. He hadn't had any action in years so I tried to seduce him, he was all too passionate about the topic and I threw him onto the coffee table,"

"Were the glass killed him," Grace said.

"Exactly," the woman said laughing.

"Who are you and how do you know me?"

"Everyone knows you Grace Zouch. You're one of the Guild's top assassins and you never ever leave a trace of your murders. You are the assassin that everyone wants to meet and learn from,"

"What's your Assassin ID?" Grace asked not sure if the woman could be trusted.

"Lord of Fire," the woman said smiling. "It isn't normal but I went through an arson phase a few years ago,"

Grace's mouth dropped. She had read about the Lord of Fire murders, it was the name that the police had given the killer because they were convinced only a man could do something so painful and awful to another human being. Granted it was only sex offenders, murderers and abusers that died but being burnt alive was awful.

And everyone in the assassin community knew it was the work of another assassin. Grace just had never dreamt of meeting them until now.

"I wanted to know if you believed me," the woman said taking a few steps closer.

"Your name then?" Grace asked knowing this woman was definitely a hot, sexy assassin that she was starting to like more and more with each passing moment.

"April," the woman said. "April Jewels and I was sent here by the real cult leader I fear because two assassins never get given the same case,"

Grace nodded and she looked at Ellis's body. "But why would the cult leader hire two different killers?"

"I am not a killer," April said smiling. "I am simply a facilitator of death and the various objects around me do the killing,"

Grace laughed. She really did like this woman so Grace went over to Ellis's phone, took out his phone and unlocked it with his retina.

Grace flicked through the contacts and noticed there was nothing about a cult leader. He was sending out all the information, all the orders for various murders and everything else that he had been doing for the past decade.

There wasn't a real cult leader. Ellis had simply been a paranoid old fool about his own safety.

But if that was true then who had hired her and April?

Grace whipped out a gun and pointed it at April.

"Who hired you?" Grace asked.

April shrugged. "No one. I simply wanted to meet the legendary Grace Zouch, the world's best assassin and I really wanted to ask you out on a date,"

Grace wanted to believe April was lying, trying to pull a con on her or she was playing another game with her. But there was just such a wonderful, delightful softness and gentleness in her eyes that Grace knew there wasn't.

There was no game here, no lie and nothing else. This was simply a fangirl wanting to meet her hero and Grace couldn't deny that April was so damn beautiful and she did love her sense of humour.

"Let's clean the place," Grace said.

"Why?"

Grace watched the beautiful woman as she peeled off her false fingerprints and Grace laughed because she always carried round the same thing. She wasn't sure what her own fingerprints looked like these days and Grace was convinced that April was the real thing.

And Grace knew there would be no DNA, no hair and no forensic evidence for the police to recover. Mainly because they were that good and also because she just knew the police wouldn't care once they discovered the phone.

A mass cultist and murderer was dead, no one cared and Grace was looking forward to moving and escaping London again.

And as she left the apartment with April close by her side, she was really looking forward to getting to know the hot, sexy assassin who was crazy smart, seductive as hell and clearly had a beautiful body under all those clothes.

Grace was so looking forward to exploring all those things about her, and at least all her assassin problems were solved. Her target was dead, she had met a beautiful woman and now she was free to explore a brilliant relationship just like she had always wanted.

MYSTERY SHORT STORY COLLECTION VOLUME 3

DANGERS OF OPENED WINDOWS
15th August 2022
Canterbury, England

Two months after the attack, Sean felt the anxiety afflicted him and stirred up in striking waves that seemed to smash into him for a moment before passing. He felt like the ground and the entire world would collapse around him, his chest might even explode and he was completely alone for those moments. Until the anxiety passed and everything returned back to normal. It wasn't really a way to live but at least the therapy was helping.

Sean leant against the warm wooden doorframe of his and his boyfriend Harry's bedroom with Harry an almost dangerously thin line under the thin blue silk sheets in their double bed, surrounded by some fine wooden chests of drawers, wardrobes and there was even a wooden black chest at the bottom of the bed.

Yet the roaring of Harry's snorting still managed to vibrate the spotlight-like lights in the corners of the bedroom, but Sean was just glad for any sounds coming from him. Because they all meant that the love of his life was alive, and that was all that mattered to Sean.

Sean never really did understand why his Auntie Bettie English, a private eye, had gifted them so much stuff when him and Harry moved in to help them recover after the homophobic attack. He partly supposed that it was because she felt guilty for some stupid reason, it was never her fault and it was her that had put the bastards behind bars forever.

Something rustled downstairs but Sean ignored it. It was probably just the neighbour cat after some of Bettie's tuna again.

If anything, it should be Sean's own mother and father who should feel guilty for what they didn't do. Even after Sean's mother's meltdown a few weeks ago where she confessed that she never wanted children so early anyway, Sean had wanted them to fix their issues.

But they hadn't.

Sean actually didn't mind that too much as bad as it sounded, he loved his Auntie Bettie and it was great to help out around the massive and expensive house as Bettie and her boyfriend Graham, a cop, prepared for the arrival of their twins.

The only problem with Harry being so tired after coming back from brain therapy was that it just meant he slept alone. Sean wasn't exactly a massive fan of that, because it meant him and Harry didn't have too much time for talking, making love and catching up on their days.

Yet considering that the first six months of brain therapy was the most important in making sure that Harry made a complete recovery, it was always far better to sacrifice these months with him now, than possibly lose him forever. Not that it really mattered anyway, considering Sean would love Harry no less.

"House is empty mate," someone said.

Sean froze and just focused on the thin line that was Harry under the sheets. Someone was clearly in the house, they were probably in the kitchen and making their way towards him.

Sean couldn't have them in here, what if they were going to beat him again? What if these people would finish the job of killing him and Harry? What if…

One… two… three…

Sean forced himself to take slow breaths until he counted to ten and he needed to focus. Bettie and Graham wouldn't be back for hours yet because they were in London at some big fundraising event for a charity. It was just Sean and Harry here for a while, and Sean couldn't risk waking Harry because he had another day of therapy tomorrow so he couldn't be tired for that.

Sean was alone, he had to protect his soulmate and he wasn't going to let some criminal idiots dare defile his Auntie's house.

Sean took out his smartphone and quickly texted Bettie that people were in the house. The smart thing might have been to call the police, but considering it was two police cops that had beaten him and caused Harry's brain damage. That was a last resort.

"Mate look at these pictures. That woman might be old but she's banging. Wanna wait for her to come home," someone said.

Sean's hands formed fists. How dare they talk about his auntie like that.

Sean forced his gaze away from Harry and turned

to focus on the very long bright wooden hallway with the long wooden staircase with an iron railing down at the end. There was nothing in the other rooms that shot off from the hallway that would help him.

The only thing that could help Sean now was to confront the criminals and get them to leave.

Sean carefully tipped-toed down the hallway, making sure to focus on the top of the staircase in case one of the criminals was coming up. He couldn't get caught just yet.

He couldn't entirely understand how the criminals had gotten in, granted he had left the kitchen window open because it was too hot and he had cooked himself a chicken curry, so he hated to get rid of the smell.

But surely two criminals couldn't climb in through a window?

Sean reached the top of the staircase and normally its smooth wooden features looked so stylish, calm and great. But today Sean wasn't pleased with them, they made the house look too luxurious and like the perfect target for criminals.

Sean slowly started to go down the stairs. All he needed to do was reach the bottom of the stairs and look round the right-hand corner into the living room to see what was going on.

"Mate what you wanna do if there's someone here. We got a lot of stuff to search and steal," someone said.

Now he was closer, Sean knew that the *mate* speaker (the only one he had heard so far) was definitely a young male.

"We make sure they don't tell on others. Boss wants us to make sure this bitch knows not to mess with us," a slightly older female voice said.

Sean's heart started to pound. What if they were killers? What if they were dirty cops? What if they were going to beat him so badly he was brain damaged too?

Sean's world started to spin. This couldn't be happening again. He couldn't survive another piece of trauma. Not now, not ever.

These people were going to finish him off.

Sean felt the entire house move around him like it was going to smash down on him. Killing him.

One… two… three…

This was absolutely ridiculous and Sean was going to end this now. He was not having some idiots scare his Auntie, rob her house and endanger the man he loved.

That wasn't happening.

"Well, well, well," a young woman said from the bottom of the stairs.

Damn it. This is why he hated himself and his anxiety and those stupid cops. That had made him into this incapable idiot that was useless when he was alone, and not next to his amazing Auntie.

But Sean wasn't stupid.

He didn't speak, he only focused on the young woman in front of him and most importantly how to overpower her, all whilst keeping a good few metres from her and the small pocket knife she was carrying.

She definitely wasn't the prettiest of young women with her deadly black eyes and horribly dirty blue jeans and t-shirt. She didn't look happy to be here but Sean had seen the coldness in her eyes plenty of times before.

She hated him. And he hated her.

"Get up," the young woman said.

Sean didn't react or move. She wasn't in control here and most people would focus on the small knife at this time but Bettie had made sure to teach Sean why that was always a bad idea. Focus on the person so he knew what she looked like for a description later on.

And the knife wouldn't be the first sign of trouble. It would always be the idiot holding in.

"Get up now," the young woman said.

Sean slowly nodded and he almost liked hearing the sheer amount of annoyance, rage and anger in her voice. Whoever this woman was she never wanted Sean to be here.

Sean went down the stairs and hooked a right into Bettie's beautiful living room, and normally the massive TV hanging on the white walls, the cream-coloured three-seater sofa and two armchairs centred around a brown coffee table were normally so bright and loving and comforting.

But the mere presence of the strangers seemed to make the entire room seem sadder, lonelier with a slight shade of anger. That was properly what Sean was feeling, but he was just determined to get these young idiots out of the house.

"Yo mate?" a young man said from the opposite side of the living room as he came in from the kitchen carrying real silverware.

Sean had to admit the young man was rather hot considering he was wearing tight black jeans, a loose-fitting t-shirt that highlighted how muscular he was behind it and he had longish black hair.

But now Sean had both of the idiot criminals in his sights he just knew that he had to focus and make sure both of them were captured.

"Sit," the young woman said.

Sean smiled. "I'm not a dog. What do you two want?"

Sean was a little disturbed that the young man was just staring in utter confusion at him. It was probably something to do with Sean's blond hair with stylish streaks of pink running through it, but he didn't care what this criminal scum thought of his hair. He was going to have them both suffer.

Sean felt the icy coldness of the point of a blade jab into his shoulder.

"I said sit," the young woman said. "Then I will tell you exactly what we are doing and how you are going to help us,"

Sean highly doubted that but the criminals were willing to talk so he carefully sat down on the sofa making sure to keep both of them in sight.

The young woman sat on the coffee table.

"We are here because our boss wants your auntie to leave her alone," the young woman said.

Sean was impressed that she knew he was her nephew, but given how Bettie wasn't only a private eye but the President of the British Private Investigator Federation, it was only strange that someone hired these two.

It couldn't be related to a case because Bettie had only been doing background checks constantly for the past few weeks because she was due to give birth next month.

Sean seriously doubted it was anything to do with the Federation because Bettie had been so focused on rebuilding it after all the corruption and whatnots of the last president.

"And breaking in will help you how?" Sean asked.

The young woman asked. "Our boss can get anywhere. Our boss is superior. Our boss-"

"is prob useless little old lady takes advantage of children need love, support respect," Harry said from the doorway.

Sean's heart shot into his throat. He was impressed how much better his speech was coming along. He didn't want him down here. He only wanted Harry to be safe.

The young woman grinned. "Excellent. We have the boyfriend and the nephew. The boss will be so pleased,"

Then it twigged to Sean that they were never going to rob the house. This was actually all about him and Harry and they were probably going to take them hostage or threaten them until Bettie agreed to leave them alone.

Sean admired the stupidity of their boss because he just knew that any threats made against him and Harry would be met with rage, a man hunt and strict retribution.

But Sean admired people's willingness to doom themselves.

Sean stood up. Now that he had some idea of what the two criminals wanted he just needed to break them up and weaken whatever hold the young woman had over the other one.

If he was to act then Sean needed them not to be a team.

"I know you don't respect the boy over there," Sean said pointing to the young man. "You see him as a pointless burden that your boss made you bring him along. I think he isn't the brilliant tool in the workshop,"

The young woman nodded. "Of course not. I come from a quality background not some council estate where idiots call each other *mate, bro* and *dude,*"

The young man stomped his foot. He was clearly annoyed.

Sean looked at Harry who was extremely beautiful standing there and they just winked at each other.

Sean's pretended his heart pounded. His breathing quickened. He clutched his chest.

Sean hissed and screamed and panicked.

The young woman looked shocked and panicked herself.

Sean collapsed to the sofa. Pretending to have a panic attack. Harry shouted at them.

The young woman dropped the knife.

She rushed to Sean. Leaning over him.

Sean kicked her.

Punching her in the chest.

She flew to the ground.

Sean leapt up. Jumping on top of her.

Sean pinned her down.

The young man whacked Sean in the head.

The young woman threw Sean off her.

Sean jumped up.

The moment he saw the young woman holding Harry in a headlock with the small knife kissing his neck. Sean stopped.

The young man put Sean in a headlock to (a rather pathetic one but still) and Sean just felt like he was a complete and utter failure.

He had put the love of his life in danger and for

what. His own insecurities about the corrupt police that had put him in hospital, his own anxiety and God knows whatever concerns he had that made him feel like he was the only one that could protect himself and that no one else cared about him.

Then the living room got a little brighter. No one else seemed to notice and Sean couldn't understand if the bright tones of the living rooms were actually brighter than before but they just felt like they did.

Sean just knew that something was about to happen and he really needed to distract them.

"Your boss doesn't love you you know. She might have found you on the streets or whatever but she actually hates you," Sean said.

The young woman seemed furious. Sean hated the sound of the young man's breathing in his ear.

"And you," Sean said to the young woman. "If your beginnings were so great then why were you on the street to be found?"

The young woman's hand tensed. She gestured she would kill Harry but Sean knew that would only anger her boss.

"I think you were just a jumped-up child that no one wanted and you wanted to get respect from another person that doesn't even love you," Sean said coldly.

The young woman threw Harry onto the sofa. She stormed over to Sean waving the knife about.

"I am loved. The boss loves me. She treasures me and-"

The front door exploded open.

Sean jumped back.

Smashing the young man into the wall. His head cracked on the wall.

He released Sean.

Sean spun around. Punching the man in the nose.

He collapsed to the ground.

And when Sean looked at where the young woman had been standing, he saw one of the most perfect sights he ever could have wished for, because Graham in his fine black suit was handcuffing the young woman and reading her her rights.

A few moments later after Graham had escorted the young man and woman out of the house, Sean just smiled as a very pregnant Bettie English stumbled through the front door.

Sean had to admit she did look stunningly beautiful in her large black dress that managed to make her massive baby bump seem so stylish and she simply hugged Sean and Harry.

Sean loved the amazing warmth of the hug and he was glad that they had arrived when they did, and more importantly that beautiful Harry was okay.

Then Sean noticed the evil smile on Bettie's face, and Sean looked up at the ceiling and noticed a very small black camera right above his head.

"You knew this would happen," Sean said.

Bettie shrugged as she stumbled over to the armchair.

"Didn't you think it was odd that the kitchen window didn't lock properly?" Bettie asked.

Sean hadn't even noticed.

"That created the perfect opening for them to come in. I knew you two were smart enough to stay safe until we arrived and you got us the proof we needed," Bettie said.

"Proof what?" Harry asked.

"Two days ago I ran a background check for a

government role and it highlighted that criminal gangs were trying to get jobs in the UK Government and someone was helping them,"

Sean just nodded. It was just getting too ridiculous with the Government for words.

"So after some investigating," Bettie said, "me and Graham managed to track down the extra help to an orphanage and homeless shelter in London and the owner, a little old lady I should note, had powerful friends in the government,"

Sean nodded. "This woman was doing favours for her friends by getting the vulnerable children she *cared* for to do her dirty work for her all to protect her criminal friends in the government,"

Bettie nodded.

Sean looked at beautiful Harry who was hugging him and Sean was slightly getting more and more concerned about how thin he was getting, but that was all part of the therapy process.

Sean kissed Harry's soft amazing lips quickly and then pointed to the stairs. It was a little gesture they both did when they knew the other needed to go to sleep.

Sean was never going to have Harry tired when he had a brain therapy day tomorrow, he just loved him too much for that.

Sean was about to follow Harry up when Bettie gently took his hand in hers.

"You did well today you know," Bettie said. "Your mum might not say it or be here, but I am proud of you and love you,"

Sean knew his auntie never understood the power of those words to him, but after hiding he was gay for so many years and all the bad mental health associated with it, being attacked by the people who were meant to protect everyone and now his own parents not seeming to care about him.

Those words meant everything to Sean.

Sean kissed Bettie on the head. "You're going to be an amazing mum,"

Bettie only nodded and she was probably holding back the tears (both in joy but also panic that her life was going to change forever in less than a month) and Sean simply went upstairs.

Sean might have done a great thing today that proved to him he was always more than his anxiety, past and the pain of what had happened. But there was always more to work on in the future.

Right now, he had a beautiful boyfriend to help, love and cherish and a wonderful Auntie to help with a pair of twins coming.

That would probably be a lot for most 21-year-olds to take but Sean honestly couldn't think of a better way to spend his time.

Not a single better way at all.

MYSTERY SHORT STORY COLLECTION VOLUME 3

GET YOUR FREE SHORT STORY NOW!
And get signed up to Connor Whiteley's newsletter to hear about new gripping books, offers and exciting projects. (You'll never be sent spam)

https://www.subscribepage.io/wintersignup

About the author:

Connor Whiteley is the author of over 60 books in the sci-fi fantasy, nonfiction psychology and books for writer's genre and he is a Human Branding Speaker and Consultant.

He is a passionate warhammer 40,000 reader, psychology student and author.

Who narrates his own audiobooks and he hosts The Psychology World Podcast.

All whilst studying Psychology at the University of Kent, England.

Also, he was a former Explorer Scout where he gave a speech to the Maltese President in August 2018 and he attended Prince Charles' 70th Birthday Party at Buckingham Palace in May 2018.

Plus, he is a self-confessed coffee lover!

Other books by Connor Whiteley:
Bettie English Private Eye Series
A Very Private Woman
The Russian Case
A Very Urgent Matter
A Case Most Personal
Trains, Scots and Private Eyes
The Federation Protects
Cops, Robbers and Private Eyes
Just Ask Bettie English
An Inheritance To Die For
The Death of Graham Adams
Bearing Witness
The Twelve
The Wrong Body
The Assassination Of Bettie English
Wining And Dying
Eight Hours
Uniformed Cabal
A Case Most Christmas

Gay Romance Novellas
Breaking, Nursing, Repairing A Broken Heart
Jacob And Daniel
Fallen For A Lie
Spying And Weddings
Clean Break

Awakening Love
Meeting A Country Man
Loving Prime Minister
Snowed In Love
Never Been Kissed
Love Betrays You

Lord of War Origin Trilogy:
Not Scared Of The Dark
Madness
Burn Them All

The Fireheart Fantasy Series
Heart of Fire
Heart of Lies
Heart of Prophecy
Heart of Bones
Heart of Fate

City of Assassins (Urban Fantasy)
City of Death
City of Martyrs
City of Pleasure
City of Power

<u>Agents of The Emperor</u>
Return of The Ancient Ones
Vigilance
Angels of Fire
Kingmaker
The Eight
The Lost Generation
Hunt
Emperor's Council
Speaker of Treachery
Birth Of The Empire
Terraforma
Spaceguard

<u>The Rising Augusta Fantasy Adventure Series</u>
Rise To Power
Rising Walls
Rising Force
Rising Realm

<u>Lord Of War Trilogy (Agents of The Emperor)</u>
Not Scared Of The Dark
Madness
Burn It All Down

Miscellaneous:
RETURN
FREEDOM
SALVATION
Reflection of Mount Flame
The Masked One
The Great Deer
English Independence

OTHER SHORT STORIES BY CONNOR WHITELEY

Mystery Short Story Collections
Criminally Good Stories Volume 1: 20 Detective Mystery Short Stories
Criminally Good Stories Volume 2: 20 Private Investigator Short Stories
Criminally Good Stories Volume 3: 20 Crime Fiction Short Stories
Criminally Good Stories Volume 4: 20 Science Fiction and Fantasy Mystery Short Stories
Criminally Good Stories Volume 5: 20 Romantic Suspense Short Stories

Mystery Short Stories:
Protecting The Woman She Hated

MYSTERY SHORT STORY COLLECTION VOLUME 3

Finding A Royal Friend
Our Woman In Paris
Corrupt Driving
A Prime Assassination
Jubilee Thief
Jubilee, Terror, Celebrations
Negative Jubilation
Ghostly Jubilation
Killing For Womenkind
A Snowy Death
Miracle Of Death
A Spy In Rome
The 12:30 To St Pancreas
A Country In Trouble
A Smokey Way To Go
A Spicy Way To GO
A Marketing Way To Go
A Missing Way To Go
A Showering Way To Go
Poison In The Candy Cane
Kendra Detective Mystery Collection Volume 1
Kendra Detective Mystery Collection Volume 2
Mystery Short Story Collection Volume 1
Mystery Short Story Collection Volume 2
Criminal Performance

Candy Detectives
Key To Birth In The Past

<u>Science Fiction Short Stories:</u>
Their Brave New World
Gummy Bear Detective
The Candy Detective
What Candies Fear
The Blurred Image
Shattered Legions
The First Rememberer
Life of A Rememberer
System of Wonder
Lifesaver
Remarkable Way She Died
The Interrogation of Annabella Stormic
Blade of The Emperor
Arbiter's Truth
Computation of Battle
Old One's Wrath
Puppets and Masters
Ship of Plague
Interrogation
Edge of Failure

<u>Fantasy Short Stories:</u>
City of Snow

MYSTERY SHORT STORY COLLECTION VOLUME 3

City of Light
City of Vengeance
Dragons, Goats and Kingdom
Smog The Pathetic Dragon
Don't Go In The Shed
The Tomato Saver
The Remarkable Way She Died
Dragon Coins
Dragon Tea
Dragon Rider

All books in 'An Introductory Series':
Clinical Psychology and Transgender Clients
Clinical Psychology
Careers In Psychology
Psychology of Suicide
Dementia Psychology
Clinical Psychology Reflections Volume 4
Forensic Psychology of Terrorism And Hostage-Taking
Forensic Psychology of False Allegations
Year In Psychology
CBT For Anxiety
CBT For Depression
Applied Psychology
BIOLOGICAL PSYCHOLOGY 3RD EDITION

COGNITIVE PSYCHOLOGY THIRD EDITION
SOCIAL PSYCHOLOGY- 3RD EDITION
ABNORMAL PSYCHOLOGY 3RD EDITION
PSYCHOLOGY OF RELATIONSHIPS- 3RD EDITION
DEVELOPMENTAL PSYCHOLOGY 3RD EDITION
HEALTH PSYCHOLOGY
RESEARCH IN PSYCHOLOGY
A GUIDE TO MENTAL HEALTH AND TREATMENT AROUND THE WORLD- A GLOBAL LOOK AT DEPRESSION
FORENSIC PSYCHOLOGY
THE FORENSIC PSYCHOLOGY OF THEFT, BURGLARY AND OTHER CRIMES AGAINST PROPERTY
CRIMINAL PROFILING: A FORENSIC PSYCHOLOGY GUIDE TO FBI PROFILING AND GEOGRAPHICAL AND STATISTICAL PROFILING.
CLINICAL PSYCHOLOGY
FORMULATION IN PSYCHOTHERAPY
PERSONALITY PSYCHOLOGY AND INDIVIDUAL DIFFERENCES
CLINICAL PSYCHOLOGY

MYSTERY SHORT STORY COLLECTION VOLUME 3

REFLECTIONS VOLUME 1
CLINICAL PSYCHOLOGY
REFLECTIONS VOLUME 2
Clinical Psychology Reflections Volume 3
CULT PSYCHOLOGY
Police Psychology

A Psychology Student's Guide To University
How Does University Work?
A Student's Guide To University And Learning
University Mental Health and Mindset

www.ingramcontent.com/pod-product-compliance
Lightning Source LLC
LaVergne TN
LVHW012126070526
838202LV00056B/5879